STAR WARS™

MEET THE VILLAINS

DARTH VADER

MEET THE VILLAINS

DARTH VADER

Written by
Ruth Amos

Where is Darth Vader's home?

How many times do Luke and Vader duel?

Does Vader have a family?

Why does Vader make a strange breathing noise?

How does Vader see?

Find out the answers to these questions and many more inside!

Who is this scary figure?

It is Darth Vader! He is a powerful **Sith** Lord. Darth Vader wears dark clothing and armour.

What is a Sith?

A very evil person. The Sith are an ancient group who study the **dark side** of the **Force.** The Force is an energy that flows through all living things. It can be used for good or for evil.

Who is Darth Vader's Master?

Darth Sidious. This Sith Lord is extremely **strong** in the dark side of the Force. He **teaches** Vader how to use the dark side.

What does Sidious want?

Power. Darth Sidious is the **leader** of the Empire, and he uses the title of **Emperor.** The Empire is a group that tries to take over the whole galaxy.

Is the Emperor super evil?

Yes! The Emperor is cruel and cunning. He **protects** himself with a team of fierce red royal guards. Whenever the **hooded** figure of the Emperor appears, even Darth Vader bows before him.

What is Vader's job?

To carry out the Emperor's orders. Vader checks that the Empire's projects are running **smoothly.** He also hunts down any **enemies** of the Empire.

Does he keep a close eye on Imperial officers?

Yes! Vader demands **reports** from the officers on his ship and gives them many orders. He also makes **surprise visits** to Imperial battle stations. If anything goes wrong, Vader will soon find out!

Is Darth Vader strong in the Force?

Extremely. Vader has a **deep** connection to the Force, which makes him nearly **unstoppable.** His **fierce emotions** increase his Force powers.

Which Force powers does he have?

Many! Vader uses the Force to **move objects** and even people with just his **mind.** He can also use the Force to **sense** the presence of other nearby Force-users.

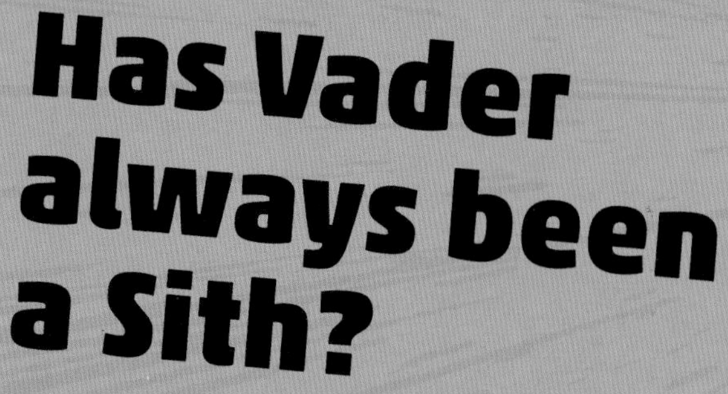

Has Vader always been a Sith?

No! Not always.

Vader was once a Jedi. His name was **Anakin Skywalker.**

Who are the Jedi?

Enemies of the Sith! The Jedi study the **light side** of the Force. They want peace and justice. They help the **Rebel Alliance** to protect the galaxy.

What is the Rebel Alliance?

A group of heroes! The brave Rebel Alliance tries to **fight back** against the Empire and gain **freedom** for everybody in the galaxy.

Where did Anakin grow up?

The desert planet Tatooine.

Anakin lived here with his mother, called Shmi. The **Jedi** spotted his **talents** and **strength** in the Force and asked him to join them.

Why did Anakin turn to the dark side?

He was scared and angry.

He had frightening **dreams** about the future. Anakin was also angry with the other Jedi. He talked about his **feelings** with a politician friend called Chancellor Palpatine.

What did Palpatine promise to Anakin?

Help. Palpatine told Anakin that the **powers** of the **dark side** could help Anakin. Palpatine **encouraged** Anakin not to trust the Jedi!

Who was Palpatine really?

He was the Sith Lord Darth Sidious! He pretended to be a good man and **tempted** Anakin to the dark side. Anakin became his Sith apprentice and took the new name of **Darth Vader.**

When does Vader have a duel on a fiery planet?

Not long after he joins the Sith.

Vader has a fierce fight with his former Jedi Master, **Obi-Wan Kenobi,** on Mustafar.

During the battle, Vader is badly injured.

Why do these old friends fight?

It's complicated! Obi-Wan realises that Anakin has fallen to the dark side. Obi-Wan **pleads** with him and tells him that Chancellor Palpatine is evil, but Vader will **not listen.**

Who is the winner?

Obi-Wan. He uses his fighting experience and lightsaber skills to wound Vader and **defeat** him. Afterwards, Darth Sidious finds the injured Vader and rescues him.

Who are these strange droids?

Medical droids. After Vader is wounded in the duel with Obi-Wan, Darth Sidious orders these skilled robots to save Vader's life. The droids fit **life-support equipment** and a black armoured **suit** onto Vader's body.

Why is Vader's helmet so important?

It keeps him alive. The helmet controls Vader's **body temperature** and allows him to speak and breathe. Its collar contains **feeding tubes.**

Why does Vader make a strange breathing noise?

He has mechanical lungs.

As air passes in and out of them, they make an eerie, **whooshing** noise. It is quite **frightening** for those around him!

How does Vader see?

His helmet contains special technology.

Vader's eyes were weakened after his duel with Obi-Wan. The helmet contains **special lenses** that protect and **sharpen** his vision.

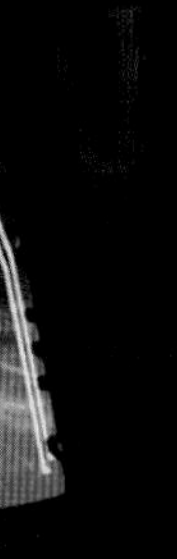

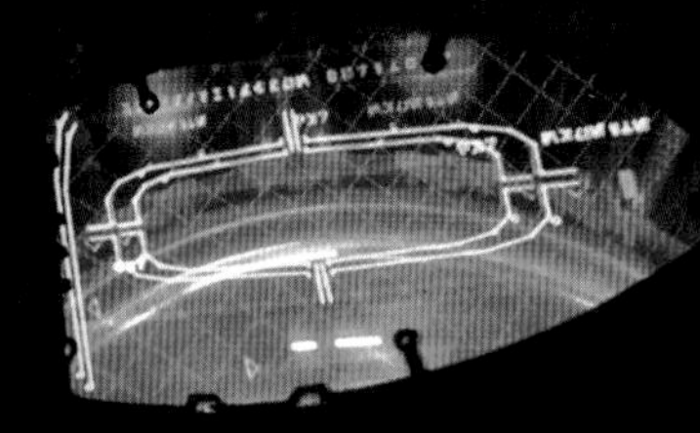

Inside view of helmet

Is Darth Vader still human?

Kind of! He used to be completely human, but when the medical droids save his life, he becomes a **cyborg.** This means that Vader is partly human and partly made of **robotic pieces.**

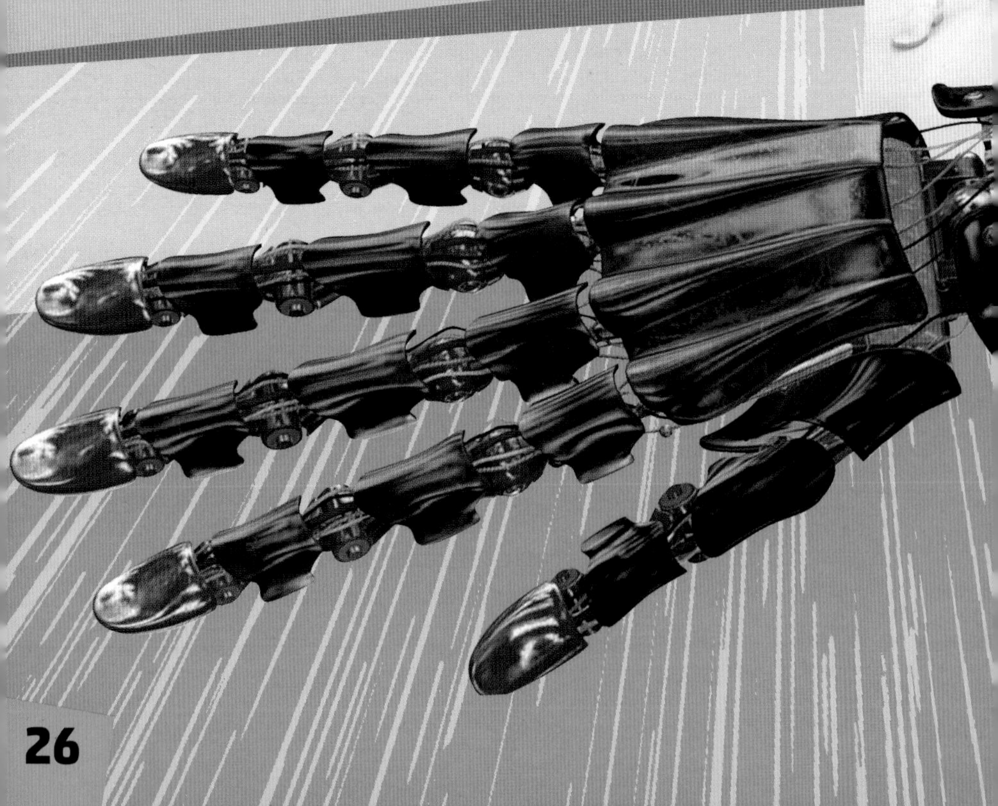

How many artificial limbs does he have?

Four. All of his arms and legs are mechanical.

Does Darth Vader have any friends?

No. Darth Vader is too busy carrying out evil plans! The Sith do not encourage **friendship** or **kindness.** They are **selfish** and often betray each other to become more powerful.

Does he have a family?

Yes, but it's tricky! When he was Anakin, he married Padmé Amidala. They had **twin babies.** After their birth, the babies were secretly given away to kind families, to protect them from Vader. He doesn't know that his children exist until they are **grown up!**

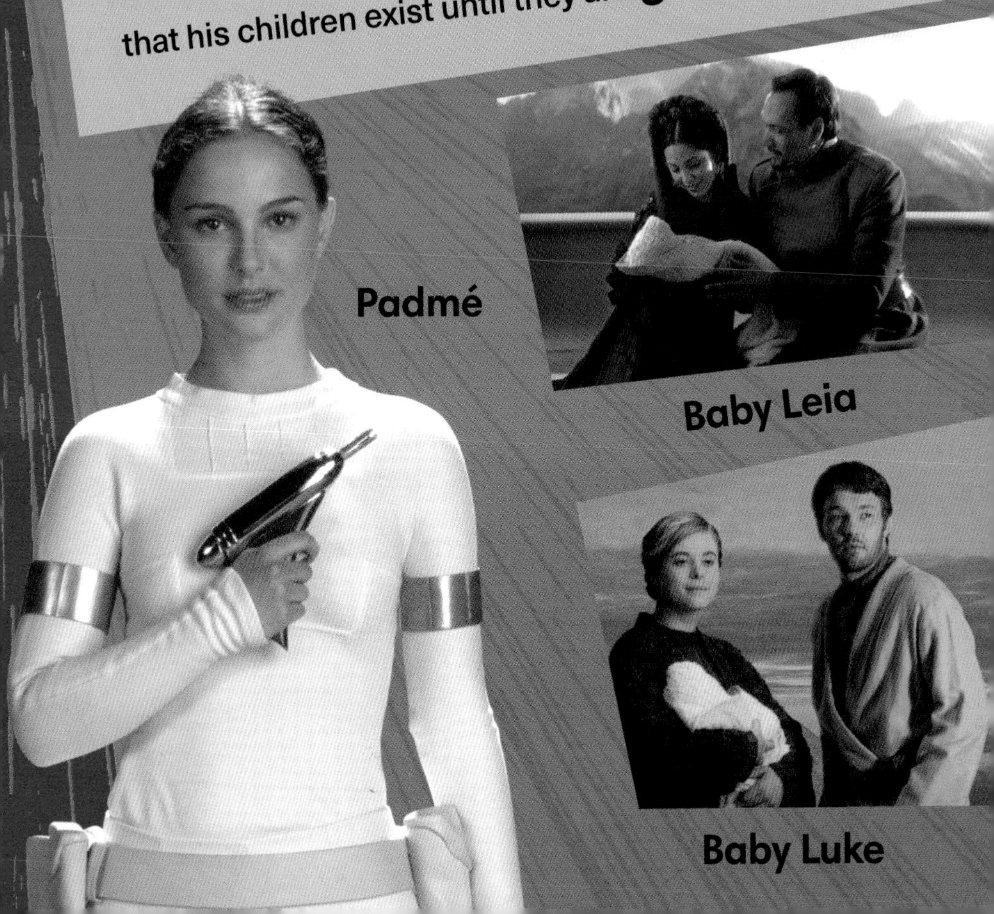

Padmé

Baby Leia

Baby Luke

Who are Vader's children?

Luke Skywalker and Leia Organa.

Luke is strong in the Force and becomes a **Jedi Knight.** Leia is a princess and a **fighter** in the Rebel Alliance.

When does Vader find out Luke is his son?

After Luke blows up the Death Star in his X-wing.

Vader senses that he is strong in the Force. Later, he finds out that Luke's surname is **Skywalker,** the same as him!

When does Luke learn the truth?

In the middle of a duel! Vader **shocks** Luke with the horrible surprise that he is Luke's father.

How does Vader realise who Leia is?

He senses it through the Force. When Vader fights Luke, he can sense Luke's worry for Leia. Vader realises that Leia is Luke's sister, and so she is his **daughter.**

Can Darth Vader fly a starship?

Yes. He's one of the best pilots in the galaxy! Vader flies his **TIE fighter** at top speeds. He performs dangerous **manoeuvres** easily.

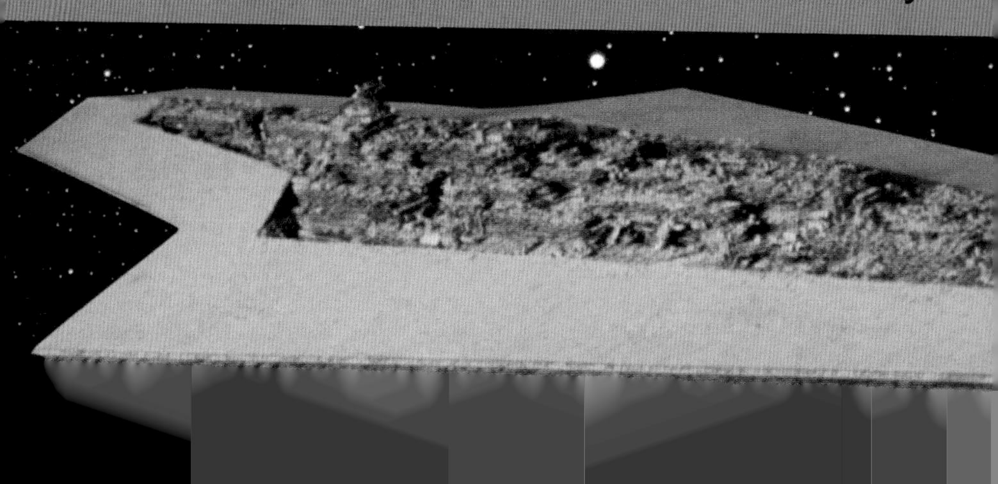

Why is his TIE fighter so special?

It has cool features. Unlike standard Imperial TIE fighters, Vader's TIE has a **defensive shield.** It also has a hyperdrive for **zooming** great distances across the galaxy at top speeds.

Does Vader have his own battleship?

Yes, the *Executor*. This Super Star Destroyer has **thousands** of crew members and carries many smaller ships.

What cool weapon is Darth Vader holding?

A lightsaber. This powerful weapon has a red blade made of **energy.** Vader uses the lightsaber like a sword to **swipe** and **strike** at his enemies.

Kyber crystal

Why is Vader's blade red?

It contains a red kyber crystal. The kyber crystal is the **power** source of the blade. The Sith have red lightsabers, while Jedi lightsabers are usually **blue** or **green.**

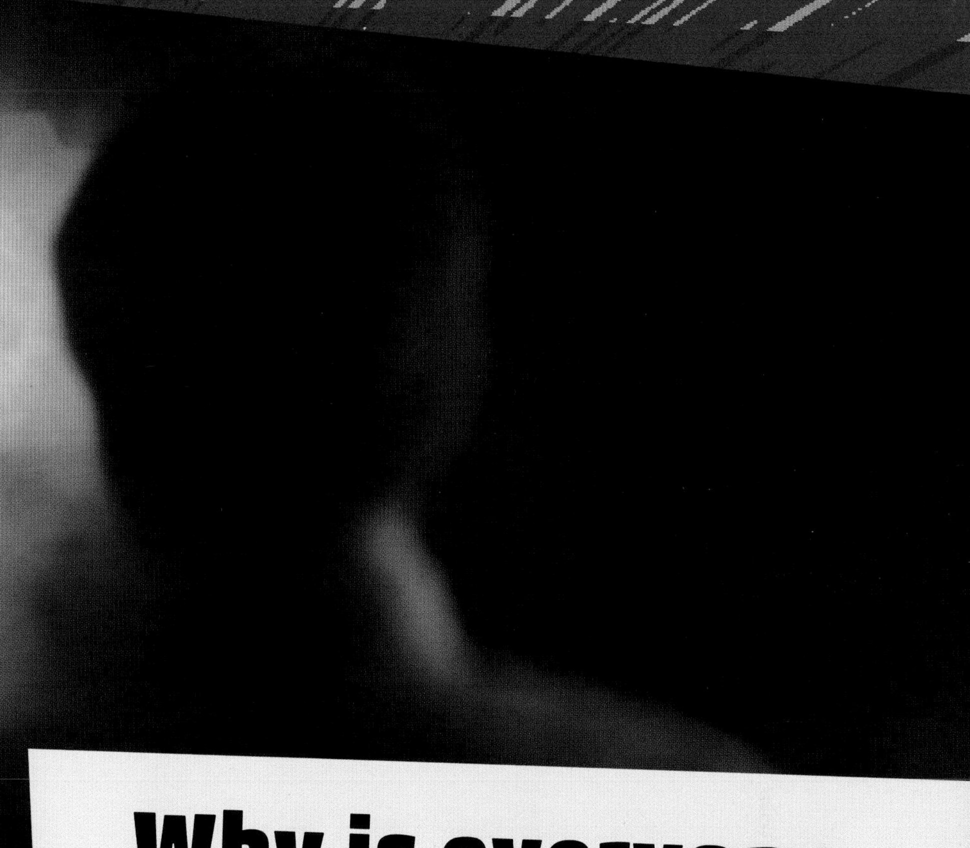

Why is everyone scared of Vader?

He has a bad temper! Vader does not often **forgive** people, and he does not **listen** to the Imperial officers' excuses. He also **looks** very frightening. When he enters a room, it is enough to terrify people!

What makes Darth Vader angry?

So many things! He does not like it when people fail to carry out his orders, **argue** with him or **question** the power of the Force!

What happens to people who disappoint him?

They are punished. Vader sometimes uses the Force to destroy Imperial officers, if they make **mistakes** or allow rebels to escape.

Who is this warrior?

Ahsoka Tano. She is a **Togruta** and comes from the planet Shili. Ahsoka was once Anakin's Jedi apprentice, but she **left** the Jedi Order. She helps the rebels of Lothal to fight against the Empire.

Does Ahsoka ever duel with Vader?

Yes, high on top of a Sith temple.

Ahsoka knows that her old master Anakin has joined the dark side. **Brave** Ahsoka tries to turn him away from the Sith, but she fails. They have an **epic** lightsaber battle!

Where is Vader's home?

On the planet Mustafar. Vader's base is a **castle** built on top of an ancient Sith **temple.** It is surrounded by **scorching** lava.

Mustafar

What does Vader get up to here?

Lots of thinking! Vader visits his castle to rest and to wait for **new** orders from his master. He also floats in a special **tank** that helps heal his injuries.

Does anyone visit him in the castle?

Yes. Vader **orders** Orson Krennic, the director in charge of building the Death Star, to meet him here. Vader warns Krennic that he is not as **important** as he thinks he is!

What big weapon does the Empire build?

The Death Star. It can destroy entire planets with its **superlaser.** But it is not as powerful as the **second Death Star,** which is even bigger! The Emperor wants this second Death Star to be indestructible!

Death Star

Second Death Star

How does Vader make the Empire work faster?

Threats! He **warns** Moff Jerjerrod, the commander of the second Death Star, that the Emperor is very **unhappy** it is not finished. Vader tells terrified Moff Jerjerrod that his troops must work faster.

Does Vader ever see his old master again?

Yes, but it ends badly! Vader and his old Jedi Master, Obi-Wan, face off on the Death Star. Vader is still angry that his **rival** won their last duel on Mustafar, many years ago. Vader declares that he is the powerful master **now!**

Who wins the fight?

It's complicated. Although Vader does destroy Obi-Wan, Obi-Wan **allows** himself to be beaten and becomes one with the Force. Heroic Obi-Wan knows this will create a **distraction.** It allows his rebel friends to escape the Death Star.

How does Vader hunt down rebels?

He uses technology. He sends Imperial **probe droids** across the galaxy to scan for the rebels' base. Vader also attaches **tracking devices** to rebel ships so he can follow them.

Probe droid

Does he ever use bounty hunters to catch people?

Yes. Vader gathers a group of bounty hunters to hunt for a famous rebel ship, the *Millennium Falcon*. He offers a **huge reward** in return for the rebels. However, they must be **alive!**

Can Vader deflect a flying blaster bolt?

He can! When Vader surprises the rebels in Cloud City, on the planet Bespin, they fight back. He uses his **Force** powers to deflect blasts from Han Solo's **blaster pistol!**

Does Vader ever make deals with people?

Yes. Vader does a deal with Lando Calrissian, the governor of **Cloud City.** Lando must **trap** his friend Han and the other rebels there, or Vader will make his life very difficult!

What is Vader's sneaky plan?

To catch Luke! Vader hopes that **loyal** Luke will come to Cloud City when he **senses** that his friends are in trouble and have been captured.

Does Vader keep his word to Lando?

No! Vader said the rebels could stay on Cloud City with Lando. **Instead,** he orders Leia, Chewbacca and C-3PO to be put onto his ship. He also hands over the prisoner Han to bounty hunter Boba Fett. Lando is **horrified!**

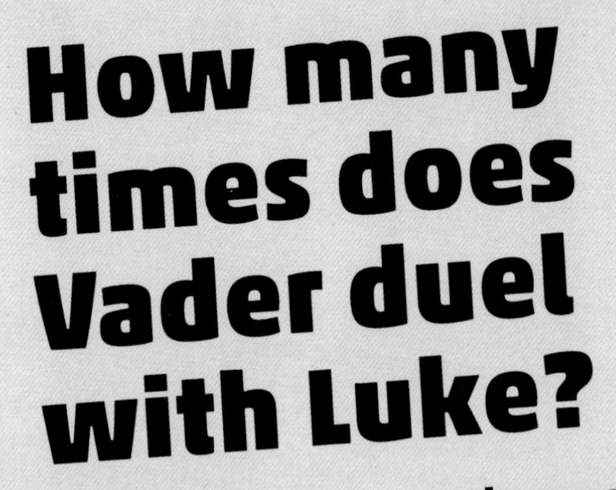

How many times does Vader duel with Luke?

Twice. Vader's first **dangerous** lightsaber duel with Luke is in Cloud City. Their next and **final** duel is on the second Death Star, in the Emperor's **throne room.**

Can Vader turn Luke to the dark side?

He can try! Vader senses Luke's power in the Force and wants him to become his Sith **apprentice.**

How does he try?

Persuasion. Vader tells Luke that they could **rule** the galaxy **together** as father and son.

Does Vader succeed?

No! Strong-minded Luke **resists** the temptation of the dark side. He is sure that he can bring his father **back** to the light side.

Is there any good left in Vader?

Yes, a little bit. He still cares for his son, Luke. Deep underneath his anger and fear, there is still **love.**

What makes him return to the light side?

Love for his son! When Luke **refuses** to join the dark side, the Emperor attacks him with **Force lightning.** Vader cannot just stand by and watch his son in danger!

How does he help Luke?

Vader destroys the Emperor! Vader's master **falls** down a deep shaft on the Death Star. Vader is wounded in the process, but he still **saves** Luke's life. Vader becomes Anakin once again! Father and son are finally **reunited.**

What happens after Anakin dies?

He becomes a Force ghost.

Anakin's life energy **lives on** through the Force, and he joins Obi-Wan and the Jedi Master Yoda as spirits. They watch over future Jedi and offer them **guidance.**

Is there peace in the galaxy?

Yes, at last! People **celebrate** the Empire's defeat with fireworks. Anakin's return to the light side has brought **balance** back to the Force. Darth Vader is no more!

Glossary

Apprentice
A person who is learning a skill.

Betray
To not be loyal to a friend or an organisation that you are part of.

Bounty hunter
Someone who tracks down, captures or kills people in exchange for money.

Cunning
Sly or deceitful.

Deflect
To make something change direction.

Epic
Long-lasting, mighty, impressive.

Force lightning
Deadly rays of energy that are used by the Sith as a weapon.

Persuasion
To cause somebody to do something or to change their mind, by using reason or argument.

Rival
An enemy or foe.

Scorching
Extremely hot.

Shaft
A vertical tunnel or passage.

Superlaser
The main weapon of the Death Star. It is powered by kyber crystals and can destroy a planet.

X-wing
A four-winged starfighter vehicle used by the Rebel Alliance.

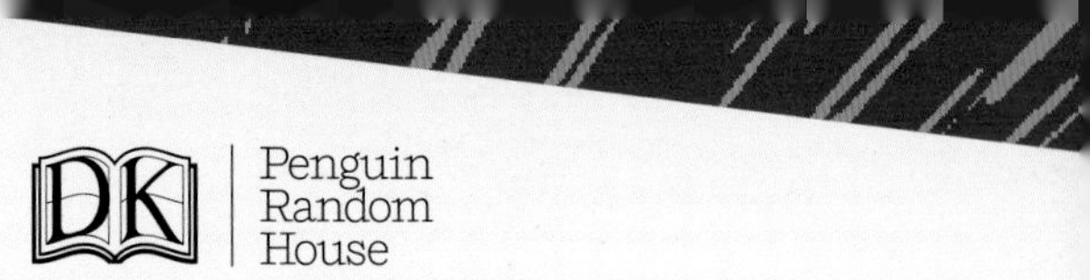

Senior Editors Ruth Amos and Emma Grange
Senior Designers Lynne Moulding and Clive Savage
Project Art Editor Jon Hall
Designers David McDonald and Stefan Georgiou
Senior Pre-Production Producer Jennifer Murray
Senior Producer Jonathan Wakeham
Managing Editor Sadie Smith
Managing Art Editor Vicky Short
Publisher Julie Ferris
Art Director Lisa Lanzarini
Publishing Director Simon Beecroft

DK would like to thank: Sammy Holland, Michael Siglain, Troy Alders, Leland Chee, Pablo Hidalgo and Nicole LaCoursiere at Lucasfilm; Chelsea Alon at Disney Publishing; Jess Tapolcai for design assistance; and Lori Hand and Jennette ElNaggar for editorial assistance.

First published in Great Britain in 2019 by
Dorling Kindersley Limited
80 Strand, London WC2R 0RL
A Penguin Random House Company

10 9 8 7 6 5 4 3 2 1
001-315151-May/2019

A CIP catalogue record for this book is available from the British Library.

ISBN: 978-0-24139-208-9

Printed in China

A WORLD OF IDEAS:
SEE ALL THERE IS TO KNOW

www.dk.com

www.starwars.com